OUT THERE

BY TOM SULLIVAN

BALZER + BRAY

An Imprint of HarperCollins Publishers

Balzer + Bray is an imprint of HarperCollins Publishers.

Out There
Copyright © 2019 by Tom Sullivan
All rights reserved. Manufactured in China.
No part of this book may be used or reproduced in any manner whatsoever without written permission except in the case of
brief quotations embodied in critical articles and reviews. For information address HarperCollins Children's Books, a division
of HarperCollins Publishers, 195 Broadway, New York, NY 10007.
www.harpercollinschildrens.com.
ISBN 978-0-06-285449-0.
The illustrations for this book were collaged together using pens, pencils, markers, paint, and Photoshop.
Typography by Tom Sullivan and Dana Fritts
19 20 21 22 23   SCP   10 9 8 7 6 5 4 3 2 1
❖
First Edition

This book is dedicated to anyone who's ever
looked up at the stars with wonder

Have you ever looked up at the night sky?

Yeah, of course—hasn't everyone?

But have you *really* looked? Past the moon
and the other planets, deep into outer space?

And have you ever wondered if there
is anybody else out there?

Yeah! There could be creepy extraterrestrials
with big heads, watching us. . . .

What about evil robots with tentacle arms?

*Or maybe there are cool aliens with blasters,
and planets with futuristic cities.*

What if instead of all that, though,
there is a world out there somewhere
that is just like ours?

It could be filled with the strangest creatures.

And cute ones, too!

There might even be intelligent life.

Just like us, only different.

Maybe they're obsessed with technology, like we are.

Or maybe they're not.

There might be places where they've ruined their planet.

And places where they've kept it clean.

Places where they're kind.

And places where they're mean.

There could be places just like here,
with families just like ours.

Other people out there on a planet,
who call the universe their home.

I mean, if space is as big as they say it is, we can't be the only ones who live here, right?

Wait a second—you don't actually believe in aliens . . . do you?

All the strange creatures on pages 14–15 are real animals on our own planet!

1. Goblin shark
2. Portuguese man-of-war
3. Flapjack octopus
4. Cassowary
5. Blobfish
6. Black rain frog
7. Narwhal
8. Golden snub-nosed monkey
9. Gerenuk
10. Axolotl (a.k.a. Mexican walking fish)
11. Long-eared jerboa